An Interactive Emotion Mat

How is Peter Feeling?

Cameile Henry and George Ashley

WestBow Press books may be ordered through booksellers or by contacting:

WestBow Press
A Division of Thomas Nelson & Zondervan
1663 Liberty Drive
Bloomington, IN 47403
www.westbowpress.com
844-714-3454

Interior Image Credit: Mark Henry

ISBN: 978-1-6642-9521-6 (sc)
ISBN: 978-1-6642-9522-3 (hc)
ISBN: 978-1-6642-9523-0 (e)

Library of Congress Control Number: 2023905017

Print information available on the last page.

WestBow Press rev. date: 8/23/2023

WestBow
PRESS®
A DIVISION OF THOMAS NELSON
& ZONDERVAN

To the reader,

Sharing the experience of reading a book takes you on a wonderful literary journey of endless possibilities. This book invites you to use what you see and understand from Peter's perspective to identify his emotions as you join him on his first day of school. You will see blanks. What you need to do is fill in the blank by identifying the emotion you think Peter is experiencing.

We hope you enjoy reading the book as much as we enjoyed creating it for you.
—Cameile, George, and Mark

Thanks to those who believe wishes can happen with the stars on earth and in the sky. A special appreciation to my son, who is my inspiration, and to children, who are my motivation.
—CH

It was the first day of school, and Ms. Porcupine was helping Peter get ready for his special day. Peter was feeling a little _____.

Peter's mom hugged him and said, "I know you are feeling _____, and that's OK. Going to a new school may be scary at first, but each day can be a new adventure. You will see Curtis. He is in your class, and maybe the two of you can hang out together on your first day of school. Now let's walk to the bus stop together."

Peter's mom asked, "How do you feel about taking the bus?"

As Peter slowly put on his shoes, he thought about his mother's question. "I feel _____, but if Curtis is there, I might feel better."

Together, Peter and his mom walked to the bus stop. Peter saw Curtis. "Hi, Curtis. Let's sit on the bus together," said Peter.

"I don't feel like it today," said Curtis.

Peter felt _____. He didn't know what to do.

His mom gave him an extra-tight hug, and he felt a little bit better but was still feeling _____.

When he got on the bus, all the seats were already filled, and he had to sit on the bumpy seat near the wheel. He bumped his head all the way to school, which made him feel _____.

When the bus arrived at the school, Peter saw a big building, and standing in front was his smiling teacher. Mr. Swordhammer greeted all the children with a warm smile and asked them to line up so they could walk into the school safely. Peter wanted to be the first in line, but Mr. Swordhammer did not hear him because all the children were talking excitedly. Peter had to go to the back of the line, and that made him feel _____.

Peter walked slowly into the classroom and found his desk. He slumped into his seat and put his head down. He was remembering what his mother said. Going to a new school may be scary at first, but each day can be a new adventure. Then Peter felt someone tap him on his back. It was Parinder.

"You are sitting in my seat! Can't you read?"

Peter felt _____. He was sure the name on the desk was his. He looked again and saw he had made a mistake; it was Parinder's name on the desk. Everyone looked at Peter. Peter felt _____. All the children began laughing.

"Peter can't read!" they shouted.

"I can read!" said Peter. His voice was loud, and then something happened. Peter's heart started to beat faster, his hands got sweaty, and he started to breathe faster. Then Peter's spines lifted. Peter was feeling _____. When Peter felt _____, his spines straightened out , because he is a porcupine. Peter didn't know what was going on. He had so many feelings that he felt like he would _____.

The children felt _____. They had never seen anything like that before.

Mr. Swordhammer shouted, "Please calm down, Peter!"

But that only made Peter feel _____, and his quills got bigger. Peter wanted his mom; he wanted her hugs to help him feel better.

Mr. Swordhammer slowly walked over to Peter, and using a calm and gentle voice, he said, "Peter, I can see you might be feeling _____."

Peter nodded.

Mr. Swordhammer then asked, "When the children laughed, it was not the way to help you feel welcome to our class, right?"

"Right," answered Peter, and he looked straight at Mr. Swordhammer.

Mr. Swordhammer said, "Sorry, Peter, for raising my voice; that might have made you feel _____. Let's try to do this again in a way that makes you feel _____."

Mr. Swordhammer then explained to the class that laughing at someone does not make them feel welcome or included. Then Peter shared that he was new to the neighborhood and the school.

Mr. Swordhammer asked the whole class, "How can we help Peter feel welcome?"

Curtis said, "Here, Peter, this is your desk. It's beside me; we can sit together."

Parinder said, "Sorry I said you can't read, Peter. I can show you to your new locker, if you like."

Soon everyone in the class was helping Peter. Peter took a big breath, and his quills came down. As he sat at his desk, he remembered what his mother said. He smiled and thought, *Today is an adventure.* Peter felt _____ because he no longer felt that he was alone.

About the Authors and Illustrator

Cameile Henry is a professor in the Early Childhood Education (ECE) at the Sheridan Institute of Technology and Advanced Learning in Ontario, Canada. As an early childhood educator and foster parent, she has over twenty-five years of facilitating learning opportunities and environments for children from infancy to twelve years of age. She is also a consultant for educators and families in the topics of race, interpersonal communication, and resiliency in young children. Cameile enjoys performing puppet plays that enhance children's social-emotional development and encourage empowerment.

George Ashley, PhD, currently serves as a professor of social work at Eastern Kentucky University, in Richmond, Kentucky, United States. He has over thirty years of extensive experience in social work practice with children K--12. Dr. Ashley also works as a consultant, workshop, facilitator, and small-group coach for Anti-racism, Equity, Diversity, and Inclusion (ADEI) education. He has authored numerous articles both in scholarly journals and popular magazines and served as a co-editor in several books. This is Dr. Ashley's first children's book. When he is not teaching, he likes telling children stories and facilitating educational programs to inspire children to achieve their best.

Mark Henry was often found creating something artistic using paper, pencil crayons, and paint as a child. Growing up in Southern Ontario, Canada, Mark's love of nature and the beauty found in people is what he now enjoys infusing into his art pieces.

We extend our heartfelt gratitude and admiration to the dedicated **Early Childhood Educators and staff** whose unwavering passion and tireless efforts shape the daily experiences of young children and families.

Your commitment to nurturing young minds, fostering curiosity, creating a safe and enriching environment does not go unnoticed. Your impact is immeasurable, and we celebrate your dedication to ensuring that every child's journey is filled with kindness, growth, and joyful learning.

As a token of our appreciation, we invite you to enjoy this special edition of

"How is Peter Feeling? An Interactive Emotion Matching Book" – a story that mirrors your invaluable role in guiding children toward emotional understanding to enhance their holistic development.

More books available in English and French

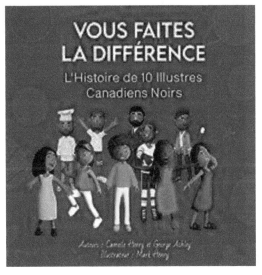

Visit us at **www.strengthenhands.com**
to receive our FREE Newsletter.

Printed in the USA
CPSIA information can be obtained
at www.ICGtesting.com
JSHW040248120923
48158JS00022B/512